W9-AQA-728

# A Dog of Flanders

This special adaptation is based on the original children's classic

by

**Marie Louise de la Ramée**

(Ouida)

ACCELERATED CHRISTIAN EDUCATION®
SCHOOL OF TOMORROW®

**Lewisville, Texas**

Adapted and printed by


Accelerated Christian Education
P.O. Box 299000
Lewisville, Texas  75029-9000


Reprinted 2013
©2000 Accelerated Christian Education,® Inc.


Dog on front cover: Photo courtesy of
Jerome M. Naftalis, M.D., P.A.


ISBN 978-1-56265-072-8
6 7 8 9 10 Printing/Year 16 15 14 13
Printed in the United States of America

# TABLE OF CONTENTS

| Chapter | Page |
| --- | --- |

# *PREFACE*

Over the years, some fine literary classics have been neglected because of their archaic expressions, unfamiliar customs, and complicated sentence structures. *A Dog of Flanders* is such a classic.

Originally written in 1872, it is not often included on contemporary reading lists for young readers. Yet this appealing story of a loving grandfather, an orphaned child, and an extraordinary and faithful dog offers a fascinating portrayal of Biblical character.

In producing this adaptation, the publisher has striven to retain the essential flavor of the original while at the same time emphasizing virtue as illustrated through the characters. Although the original author, Marie Louise de la Ramée (Ouida), emphasized the character of the dog and almost humanized him, this adaptation focuses on the people, drawing out their strengths and weaknesses.

Nonetheless, this modernization retains all the pathos and many of the tragic elements of the original writing. This classic tugs at the very core of human sympathy and reflects the impact of spiritual influences.

## *HUMBLE HOME*

Nello and Patrasche were friends and closer than brothers. Nello was a little boy; Patrasche was a big Flemish dog. They were the same age, if you count years, but Nello was still young and Patrasche was old. They had lived together almost all their lives. Both of them were orphans who had very, very little in this world. The one person who loved them and cared for them was so old that he could not do much for them. Nevertheless, the hardships Nello and Patrasche shared drew them together from the first, and it made their love grow stronger over the years.

Their home was a tiny, one-room hut on the edge of a little Flemish village about three miles (5 km) from the city of Antwerp. The village sat among spreading pastures and fields of flax. Through the broad fields ran a great canal with long lines of poplars and alders bending over its choppy waters and waving in the breeze. There were only about twenty homes in the little village. They were all humble cottages with shutters painted bright green or sky blue. Their rose red or black roofs sloped high, and their whitewashed walls shone like snow in the sun.

In the center of the village on a little moss-grown slope stood a windmill. It was a landmark that could be seen for miles around since the country was so flat. The windmill

had once been painted—sails and all—but that was over fifty years before, when it was built to grind wheat for the soldiers of Napoleon I of France. Over the years it had turned a ruddy brown, tanned by wind and weather. The proud windmill ran in fits and starts as if it had rheumatism and were stiff in the joints from age. It served the whole neighborhood, and the villagers, who were loyal to their windmill, felt disloyal if they carried their grain anywhere else to be ground.

The village had another landmark, but it received far less attention than the windmill. It was an old, gray, stone church with a tall, pointed steeple and a black bell hanging in a little belfry. The church had also been there for many years, although now it was neglected and in great need of repair. At one time the villagers had been as loyal to the church as they were to their windmill, but that had changed over the years. Still, these two landmarks—church and windmill—stood across from each other on opposite sides of the one lane that ran through the little village.

The windmill creaked and groaned in summer wind and winter blast, and the single bell of the little church rang faithfully morning, noon, and night with its strange, subdued, hollow sadness. Both landmarks seemed almost as much a part of the village as the villagers themselves, but one received many visitors, while the other had few.

Within sight and sound of both landmarks lived Nello and Patrasche in their little hut on the edge of the village. To the northeast, beyond a great plain of waving, golden grain and spreading flax, was the city of Antwerp. On a clear day, they could see the spire of the great church in Antwerp from the doorstep of their little hut.

The one-room hut was also the home of a very old man, a very poor man—old Jehan Daas. He was Nello's great-grandfather. In his youth Jehan Daas had been a soldier. He remembered the wars, which had trampled his beloved country as oxen tread down the furrows. When he left to defend his homeland, he had been a strong man; but a few years later, he had come back from the service with nothing except a wound that had left him physically disabled.

For many years Jehan Daas had lived alone, but when he reached eighty, his granddaughter died. She left him all she had. It was not worldly possessions or money. Her only legacy was something more precious—her two-year-old son. The boy could have been a great burden to the old man, who could hardly support himself, but he willingly took on the additional responsibility of caring for his young great-grandson. Hard as it was, the burden soon became welcome and gave the old man reason to live a few more years.

Nello, which was a nickname for Nicholas, thrived under his great-grandfather's care. Grandfather Jehan—as Nello affectionately addressed his great-grandfather—and the boy lived together happily in the paltry little hut. It was a very humble little mud hut indeed, but it was clean and whitewashed bright as a seashell on the outside. It stood on a small plot of fertile ground where they grew beans and herbs and pumpkins. Nello and his great-grandfather were poor, terribly poor. Sometimes they did not even have food to eat. Certainly, they never had enough.

In spite of their difficulties, the two had a happy home full of love. The old man was very gentle and good to his great-grandson, and the little boy was a handsome, well-behaved, honest child. Although the old soldier and his great-grandson had very little on this earth, they never forgot to thank their Heavenly Father for giving them what He had promised—food and raiment.

A wonderful boon did come their way one day. It was Patrasche. They praised God for sending such a blessing. After having him with them, they could not imagine a time without him. Aside from the precious Book on the shelf, he was the most important and valued possession they owned.

Without Patrasche they would have had no money or way to make a living, and they would have had no food.

He was their means of support as well as their protector. He was also an invaluable companion. He was strong and smart, and he worked hard. His worth really could not be measured in money. So, poor as they were, they were a contented household—Grandfather Jehan, the old man; Nello, the little boy; and Patrasche, their faithful and adored dog.

## *DOG OF FLANDERS*

Patrasche truly was a marvelous dog. He was a dog of Flanders—one of that special breed with long, black hair. His bones were heavy and sturdy. His ears stood erect like those of a wolf, and his legs bowed in a wide stance. He was the kind of dog whose ancestors had been hard-working, faithful dogs for generations. They were slaves to their masters, and they thrived without complaint under harsh treatment and conditions.

The dogs in Patrasche's bloodline had always strained under heavy loads and chafed in harnesses around the villages and towns of Flanders. Patrasche, until he came to the little hut, was no different. When not much more than a pup, he was harnessed to a cart and taught to pull heavy loads.

At thirteen months, Patrasche became the property of a peddler. The man was a drunkard and a brute, who forced Patrasche to pull heavy wares all over the countryside during long days. He gave the dog only mean treatment and never spoke a kind word. Patrasche became used to cruel, unkind words as well as blows from his owner's stick or whip. In his master's eyes, Patrasche was just a piece of property. He received no love and very poor care. His life was the most miserable imaginable. It was good that Patrasche was so strong, or he might have died under the extreme treatment.

This unhappy existence continued for two long, dreary years. Then a terrible, yet wonderful, thing happened. One especially hot summer day, master and dog-slave were traveling one of the straight, dusty, unlovely roads that led to the city of Antwerp. That day Patrasche's cart was piled high with heavy metal wares and pottery. His owner sauntered on without taking any notice of him—except to crack the whip over his tired back. The peddler stopped several times to refresh himself but never allowed Patrasche to rest for even a moment. He would not even let him drink the stale water of the canal. Instead, the poor dog was forced to go on under the pitilessly hot noonday sun.

The owner was truly a wicked man. He had not given Patrasche anything to eat for a full day, and even worse he had not allowed him to have a drink for nearly twelve hours. Finally, blind with dust, sore with blows, and totally exhausted from pulling the heavy cart, Patrasche staggered and foamed a little at the mouth and then fell to the ground.

He lay in the middle of the dusty road under the glaring sun, sick and motionless as if dead. Did the master care or come to his aid? No, the only treatment he administered was kicks, hateful words, and blows with a heavy oak club.

Such treatment was not new to Patrasche. The heartless man often rewarded his faithful dog this way. This time, however, his cruelty had gone beyond what Patrasche's mind and body could bear. As a result, the big dog lay in the road as if dead. Frustrated, the peddler screamed at him to get up and kicked him in the ribs, but poor Patrasche did not hear or get up. Assuming that his slave must be dead and no longer worth any attention, the brutal master jerked off the harness and kicked the silent body into the grass. Then he began pushing the cart up the road himself, all the while muttering and groaning. For all he cared, the ants could sting poor Patrasche and the crows could pick at him as at any other dead carcass.

The peddler headed to a nearby town. It was fair time, and he was hoping to make a good profit selling his wares. He was angry that, since Patrasche was not able to pull the heavy cart, he would have to push it himself. He did not turn around or give a second thought to his faithful dog. If he had ever heard the Scriptural proverb about regarding the life of his beast, he certainly did not intend to heed it. He was not going to waste time or resources to do anything to help Patrasche. Getting to the fair and making money were the only thoughts in his greedy, selfish mind.

Because of the fair, many people passed by on the road, but none stopped. If they saw Patrasche lying in the grass, they turned their heads and passed on by. "Just a dead dog," some muttered. They all acted like the Pharisee and Levite who passed by the wounded and dying Jewish man on the road to Jericho.

One good Samaritan came along, though. It was Grandfather Jehan. He was bent, lame, and very feeble. He was not going to the fair because he was too poor for such frivolity and waste of time and money. When he saw Patrasche, he stopped; then he kneeled down in the grass and weeds at the side of the road. With kind eyes he looked at the poor, motionless form of Patrasche. Little Nello, who was with Grandfather Jehan, was only about five years old. In contrast to his pale, white-haired great-grandfather, Nello's rosy cheeks, blond, wispy hair, and dark eyes were the very picture of health and vigor. When Nello saw the poor animal in the grass, he squatted down and patted the big head. "Poor doggy," he said.

Neither Grandfather Jehan nor little Nello could turn their backs on the helpless animal. In their little cart, they dragged Patrasche's almost lifeless body home to their little hut, which was not far away. They put him on some soft, old rags and poured cool water down his parched throat. Both Nello and Grandfather Jehan eagerly listened for his breathing to assure themselves that Patrasche was still alive. He finally began to revive, and in a few days, he responded to their loving care by getting back up on his feet. Soon it appeared that in time he would again be well and strong, but it would take many weeks for him to entirely regain his strength and spirit.

While Nello and his great-grandfather nursed Patrasche back to health, they became very fond of the big dog. The hut had been a rather lonely place. Now, with Patrasche there, the loneliness was gone. Old Grandfather Jehan seemed a little less bent, and Nello became a happy, bubbly child. When Patrasche got better and let out his first loud, hollow, broken bay, they laughed and clapped their hands and almost cried with joy. It was a sure sign that the big dog would fully recover. Nello hugged Patrasche's neck and buried his face in the soft black fur.

For Patrasche, the hut was a strange but wonderfully pleasant place, and it was the best hospital any animal could hope to have. Every day, instead of the mean, hateful words of a cruel master, Patrasche heard only the soft voice of Grandfather Jehan and loving words from Nello. Soft brushing, patting, and stroking replaced kicks and blows. If a dog could think like a person, he might have thought that he had died and gone to Heaven. Whether it was love or trust or just the natural response of a dog when treated kindly, Patrasche adopted his new family loyally.

Gentleness and kindness are amazing medicines. It was not long before Patrasche began to realize that Nello and Grandfather Jehan were not going to scream at him, hit him, kick him, or mistreat him in any way. They gave Patrasche the best accommodations their home could provide. He had one whole corner where he slept on a heap of dry grass. He was as grateful as a dog can be, and his loyalty grew every day. He lay for hours watching his new masters. One can only guess what thoughts went through his head. When he was strong again, he would find a way to show his gratitude and devotion. His spirit was getting restless. He could not just lie around the hut forever—no matter how comfortable he was.

## MAKING A LIVING

Being an injured old soldier, Grandfather Jehan had no better way to make a living than to limp around to several neighbors who owned cows and carry the milk to town for them in a little cart. They allowed him to do this mostly out of pity, but he was grateful to have some income, even if it was pitifully little. So, while the neighbors stayed at home caring for their gardens, their cows, their poultry, or their fields, Grandfather Jehan toiled to provide for himself and Nello. Because he was eighty-three and handicapped as well, this was very hard work. He and Nello took the milk to Antwerp, nearly three miles (5 km) from their humble hut. The trip sometimes became long and tedious. Nello often skipped off after a butterfly or some other attraction, and Grandfather Jehan had to rest quite often. It took most of the day for them to go and return.

Patrasche watched Grandfather Jehan and Nello come and go each day with interest. Then, one day as he lay in the sun with Nello petting and fussing over him, he watched intently as Grandfather Jehan worked arranging his cart. Patrasche seemed to feel a tugging within.

The next morning, before the old man had touched the cart, Patrasche got up and walked to it, positioning

himself between the handles. As plainly as he could, he was trying to show that he wanted to work for the man and boy who had saved his life and who continued to share their daily food with him. Grandfather Jehan did not want to put him in the harness because he thought it was cruel to treat a dog that way. Patrasche was persistent, and when Grandfather would not harness him to the cart, he tried to pull it with his teeth.

Finally, Grandfather Jehan relented. He made a harness that allowed Patrasche some freedom and did not bind him as he pulled the cart. Patrasche, now well and healthy, was very happy and satisfied. He was doing what he was born to do, and he was receiving food, love, and gentle treatment in return.

When winter came, cold and harsh, Grandfather Jehan was very grateful he had not turned his back on the dying dog on the side of the road. He considered it God's special blessing and provision in his time of need. He was getting older and growing feebler all the time. Truthfully, he did not know how he could have continued to pull the load of milk cans over the snow and through the deep ruts in the mud had it not been for hard-working Patrasche.

Compared with the way his old master had treated him, Patrasche thought this work of pulling milk cans on the little cart was easy. In fact, he thoroughly enjoyed it. He loved to be hitched to the little green cart with its bright brass cans. Joyfully, he worked by the side of the cheerful little lad, who adored him, and the gentle old man, who spoke kindly to him and praised his work.

Since he was young and strong, Patrasche's work was usually done by three or four in the afternoon. After that he was free to do as he pleased—to stretch himself, to sleep in the sun, to wander in the fields, to romp with Nello, or to play with his fellow dogs. No dog could have had a better life or have been happier.

For a while, Patrasche seemed to feel some anxiety about encountering his old master, but as the days passed, he became more at ease. Grandfather Jehan had similar thoughts about one who would so cruelly abuse a dog, but these fears eventually drifted away. What they did not know was that there was no need to worry. The man, being a drunkard, had reaped the wages of his sins and had been killed in a drunken fight. No one came after Patrasche or disturbed his happy new life. What a happy home he had with Nello and Grandfather Jehan!

Time passed, and Grandfather Jehan grew older and weaker. Finally, in the winter he became so paralyzed with rheumatism that it was impossible for him to go out with the cart anymore. Nello, now eight years old, gladly took over the job. He had learned responsibility, even though he was still a young boy. From house to house he traipsed, picking up the milk and running along beside the cart as Patrasche trotted it to town. After he delivered and sold the milk, Nello brought the money back to each house. He was honest, trustworthy, and polite. People admired this and welcomed his business.

Nello and Patrasche together were a picture to behold. Typical of many children of his country, Nello had dark, grave, tender eyes and a ruddy face framed in blond curls. He wore wooden shoes with stockings up to his knickers and a long-sleeved blouse that flapped in the breeze. Skipping merrily along beside the green cart with its brass milk cans and accompanied by the big, black dog, he looked as bright and happy as any child in prosperous Antwerp.

Nello and Patrasche did their work so well and with such joy and contentment that, when summer came and Grandfather Jehan was feeling better, he still let them pick up the milk and make the trip to town each day. That allowed him, in his old age, to sit in the doorway of the little hut and soak in the warm sunshine. It was a joy to watch the two, whom he loved most on this earth, work together so well.

While they were gone, he could meditate on the blessings God had given him. He especially thanked God for young

Nello, who brought so much joy to his old age. Had God not provided that companionship, he would surely have died from loneliness. Now he would starve without Nello's willingness to do the work that put food on their humble table. As the old man praised his Heavenly Father, he dreamed of the wonderful home and glory soon to be his as a child of God. He had known pain and hard work and sorrow for years; but he knew his Saviour would call him home soon. Only one thing concerned him—what would happen to Nello and Patrasche when he was gone?

When the boy and dog returned each day, Patrasche was turned loose to go his doggy way, and Nello told his great-grandfather about the day's activities. His customers, for the most part, were kind, and some were very generous. At supper, Grandfather Jehan, Nello, and Patrasche all sat down to their meal of rye bread and milk or soup. They had more to eat than they had ever had, thanks to God's goodness in sending them a big, strong, faithful dog that pulled the little cart to town each day.

As the months and years passed, the lives of Nello and Patrasche were very happy and blessed. Grandfather Jehan's concern turned to peace, knowing that God would continue to watch over his great-grandchild. He was glad that Nello would have Patrasche; he would otherwise be an orphan.

## THE LAND, THE PEOPLE

The three in their poor little hut were always glad when spring and then summer came. To most, Flanders was not a pretty country, especially around Antwerp. A few flowers bloomed, but field upon field of flax and grain retreated in dull monotony. Ribbons of pastures and plowed fields followed each other in unending repetition. Except for distant church bells ringing at their appointed times of the day, few new sounds broke the constant voices of the wind and the choppy waters of the canal.

The only change of scenery might be a farmer carrying a load of sheaves in his arms or a woodsman bearing his ax on his shoulder. The countryside seemed boring and uninviting, especially to any who lived in lush mountainous country or to those with an artistic flair.

Nevertheless, Flanders was a very fertile land, flat and wide to the horizon. Along the canals and streams, flowers grew and trees rose tall and green on the banks. Otherwise, the canals held little interest. Great barges glided down them with their huge hulls black against the sun. Their varied, colored flags waved gaily against the trees.

All these wide-open spaces and green fields were beautiful to Nello and Patrasche, though, for it was their home. They could ask for nothing better after a hard day's work than to lie in soft grass beside the canal and watch the big vessels drift by. They seemed to carry the smell of the sea and add to the fragrances of a country summer.

True, in the winter it was harder. Nello and Patrasche had to rise while it was still dark and bitterly cold, and they seldom had what could be considered a hearty breakfast. The hut was little more than a shed. In warm weather it looked pretty with vines and blossoms covering it. When nights were cold, however, the wind pushed through and chilled the dark room inside because the hut had many holes in its walls. Sometimes the floor flooded and then froze.

Both the little village nearby and the countryside were bleak and dreary. The ground was frozen and cold, and snow covered the icy streets and paths. Nello's thin coat and cap offered little protection against the sharp wind, and his red fingertips poked through holes in his worn gloves. Blowing snow sometimes blinded him while he trudged along beside Patrasche. The rough, frozen ground often cut and bruised the dog's feet. Nevertheless, the two had to do their job, no matter how hard or uninviting, if they wanted to eat.

Yet, in spite of hardships, neither of them complained. Nello in his rough, wooden shoes and big, lumbering Patrasche on frozen paws trotted bravely together over the icy fields to the jingling of the bells on the leather harness. Sometimes, in the streets of Antwerp, some housewife would bring them a bowl of soup and a handful of bread, or a kind store owner would throw sticks of wood for fuel into the little cart as the two made their way homeward. One woman in their own village often told them to keep for themselves some of the milk they carried for her. When wonderful things like these happened, Nello would happily run over the snowy paths and lanes, through the dusk of evening, and burst through the door of their little home with shouts of joy.

Young Nello, having known nothing but this life and thinking it not much different from that of others, was thankful for God's blessings. Patrasche, on the other hand, when he saw other dogs like himself being treated cruelly and having little to eat and no shelter from the cold, remembered how his life had been before. Yes, he was often very hungry when he lay down at night. He had to work in the merciless heat of summer and the chilling cold of winter, but his life was good for a dog. Many times his feet were tender with wounds from the sharp, jagged edges of the frozen roads. The loads were heavy, and certainly he would have liked to run in the fields instead of being harnessed to a cart. Yet he did his job out of devotion to the two who had shown him so much kindness.

The only time Patrasche felt uneasy was when he was near one of the old churches of Antwerp. Perhaps it was how dark, dreary, and lifeless they were, or maybe it was the bells that often rang from their high steeples and hurt Patrasche's ears.

One of these great churches was a tribute to a long-dead hero of Antwerp—the great artist Peter Paul Rubens. The old church was a memorial to him for his contribution to art. Though now long dead, Rubens helped make Antwerp a famous city.

It is good for a city and a country to have heroes, but still they are only men. If they recognize that their gifts and talents are God-given, they will want their work to bring glory and honor to Him and not to themselves. Men can build great monuments to honor their heroes; but in the end a monument to a person, however great he may have been, can never bring new life to those who visit it. Those who visited the great church in Antwerp to see Rubens' famous paintings of Christ needed to know and honor, not Rubens, but the One Whom Rubens tried to picture on canvas.

One day as Nello and Patrasche passed the great church in Antwerp—glistening white in the sun and with spires soaring high into the blue sky—some people were coming out. The boy and dog stopped and watched them for a few moments. Their heads were bowed and their faces pale. They left silently, sadly. Nello understood why. He, too, had gone into the church in the past with Grandfather Jehan. They had both left the same way these people left—sad and empty-feeling inside.

Nello knelt and stroked Patrasche. "They are sad," he explained, "because they are seeking for peace and for hope. They will not find it in this church."

Like those poor souls, Grandfather Jehan and Nello had sought for peace there also. They had paid the few coins— going without food to do so—just to see the two veiled pictures painted by Rubens that hung inside. The man in black robes and silver chains promised that it would help. He said they should look at the picture of the Saviour placed on the Cross and then at the other picture showing His dead body being taken down from the Cross before His resurrection. Like the other people, they thought just looking at the pictures would somehow fill their emptiness. It did not. No picture or statue or altar—no matter how magnificent—can take away sin and give one peace.

That was before Nello and Grandfather Jehan had visited the old, gray church in the village—the one across from the ruddy brown windmill. It was small and tumble-down. The pews were rough and hard, the floor bare and cold. Not much sunlight came through the narrow, old windows, and

31

the walls badly needed paint. No beautiful pictures hung there. The loveliness was something felt rather than seen. When the small group met there and the pastor humbly preached, it was as if God spoke. Nello and Grandfather Jehan had found peace and hope there. They had felt the burden of sin lifted, and it had cost them nothing.

"The old church across from the windmill—that is where we found what we were looking for, Patrasche," said Nello.

Yes, it had happened there one lovely Easter morning. Grandfather Jehan had been too stiff and too sore to walk to the great church in Antwerp. Even in their village, he could hear the music from the bells in the high steeples of Antwerp, but he could not get there. It broke his heart. He had held back a few coins to put in the box, but he could not go. That was when the one small bell in the old, gray church across from the windmill began to ring, inviting Easter worshipers. Only a very few accepted the welcome. Most had already gone to Antwerp or did not want to be bothered with church anywhere.

"I cannot walk to Antwerp, Nello," Grandfather Jehan had said, "so we will go to the old church in our village. That will be better than nothing. I just trust my coins will be well spent there. Perhaps some peace will be mine, even if my stomach is empty for it."

They had gone, and there they heard for the first time what God truly said about sin. The coins, so precious, were not enough to pay the price for forgiveness of sin and for real peace within. It had to be paid in blood. Grandfather Jehan could not pay; Nello could not pay; for God's Son had already paid with His precious blood.

Now, as Nello and Patrasche stood watching the worshipers leaving the great Antwerp church, Nello confided, "We no longer come here to see the pictures, but I still admire the great artist who made this town remembered." Indeed, Nello spent much of his time dreaming of being a great artist himself. He was very poor and he could not read or write, but he had a gift from God. The gift was in his head and in his fingers. It was the gift of art.

# THE GIFT

No one knew Nello was gifted. He really did not know it himself, and that was good. If he had known, he might have been tempted to become proud. God would have no glory then, and after all, that is why God gives each of us special gifts—to bring glory to Himself. If others had been interested, they might have noticed what Patrasche saw. Nello drew pictures. In his pictures, he captured flowers and birds, trees and butterflies. He caged them by drawing them on stones because he did not have paper. For charcoal and brush, he used whatever would make a mark—a soft stone or a tiny piece of discarded chalk. It did not matter. Nello loved to draw. The evening glow of a sunset inspired him as he and Patrasche sat on the riverbank and watched the sun sink below the horizon. The rosy coming of dawn, to him, was breathtaking.

He never talked about his artistic passion to Grandfather Jehan because the old man had no money to buy him paints or pencils or canvases. Indeed, he could not afford to buy him even a few pieces of chalk or charcoal. Nello never asked his great-grandfather for these things, but he did talk with his Heavenly Father about them. In fact, he often prayed so earnestly that tears came, rolled down his cheeks, and dropped onto Patrasche's fur. Nello liked talking with his Heavenly Father because he knew his Heavenly Father heard and would answer his prayers.

One day Grandfather Jehan surprised Nello. "You are nearly twelve now—almost a man. I could die content, Nello, if I knew that when I am gone you could earn a moderate living and own this hut and the little plot of ground around it. I want you to work hard and be respected by your neighbors. It will make my heart glad, and it will please our Lord. He has given us so much. He has provided for us all these years, and it is much more than we deserve. He is such a good God. You must always honor Him, Nello."

Nello said nothing. He loved his great-grandfather and would never do anything to hurt him, but in his heart he really did not care to work the soil. Yes, he wanted to keep the hut and the land and he wanted his neighbors to respect him, but what he wanted to do more than any of these was draw and paint. He knew artists, like Rubens, made their living by painting. He wanted to be one of them. He wanted to use his gift, which he was only beginning to realize he had, for God's glory and for his own livelihood.

Nello confided in Patrasche. He whispered his ideas and dreams in Patrasche's ears at night before he went to sleep. He discussed color and light with Patrasche as they carried their neighbors' milk to town. When Patrasche saw a piece of chalk or sniffed a piece of discarded charcoal on a sidewalk or path, he stopped until his master found it. On sunny afternoons, they lay on a soft riverbank, Nello mixing clay for paint and smearing it into scenes on smooth rocks. Not even Grandfather Jehan saw these warm, glowing masterpieces—only Patrasche.

In fact, Grandfather had very little appreciation for art. Now that he was old and often bedridden, he would have been very troubled by Nello's thoughts and plans. He had never understood why people traveled to Flanders just to see the works of Rubens. One artist's work was just as good as another's in his eyes. Tilling the soil was a worthwhile profession. Scratching lines and daubing colors on canvas would leave a man penniless.

There was only one other besides Patrasche to whom Nello could talk about his daring fantasies. That was Alois. She lived at the old, ruddy brown mill on the grassy mound. Her father, the miller, was the most well-to-do tradesman in the village. Alois was a dainty little girl with soft features and rosy cheeks. Like many Flemish, she had dark eyes inherited from some Spanish ancestor. Years earlier, the Spanish had conquered Flanders and lived there. While Flanders was under Spanish rule, the groups mixed and their descendants had traits of both. Not only was Spanish influence seen in many faces, it was also evident in the architecture of many majestic palaces and homes. Wide arches, lovely gardens, and tile roofs were all influences from a time past.

Alois was the richest child in the hamlet. She had no brothers or sisters. Her pretty dresses never had holes in them; and, at the sweet shop, she bought as many fancy candies and treats as she could hold. When she went to church, her flaxen curls were always set off with the prettiest and laciest bows. Even though she was just ten, foolish men talked about what a good wife she would be for their sons, as if money and pretty looks made a good life's companion. Her family name and money were not important to her though, and her favorite playmates were Nello and Patrasche.

Alois was often with Nello and Patrasche. They ran in the snow, they played in the fields, they gathered daisies and blackberries, they went up to the old, gray church together, and they often sat together by the broad fireplace in the mill house.

One day Mr. Cogez, Alois' father, came by where the three were playing in the newly mowed meadow behind the mill. He was a good but somewhat stern man. What he saw disturbed him. There was Alois, his lovely little daughter, sitting in a pile of hay with the big, dark head of

Patrasche in her lap. She had made wreaths of poppies and blue flaxflowers to hang about both their necks. Beside them sat Nello, drawing their picture with a stick of charcoal on a piece of clean, smooth pinewood.

The miller stood and looked at them for a moment. His daughter was a beautiful little girl, and he loved her very much. The scene brought tears to his eyes. Nello was a good boy, but Mr. Cogez could not let Alois spend time with him. Nello was poor, and she was rich. The father had greater expectations for his daughter than having her interested in someone with no name or wealth attached to his future. As he approached, Mr. Cogez covered his true feelings by speaking roughly to Alois, telling her she should be helping her mother. Alois began to cry but obeyed her father and went inside. He then turned to Nello and, grabbing the piece of wood from Nello's hands, he scolded the young artist in a trembling voice. "Why do you fool around with such things?"

Nello's face turned red with embarrassment. Looking down, he replied, "I draw everything I see, sir."

The miller was silent. He felt somewhat ashamed for being so harsh; and, even at a glance, he could see that the picture was a good likeness of his little daughter. Then he stretched out his hand with a franc in it. "Do you think you are an artist? You can find better ways to spend your time.

However, it does look a little like Alois, and her mother would probably like it. Take this money and let me have the picture."

Nello overcame his embarrassment and looked up. It was an uncomfortable situation because he knew the miller looked down on him for being poor. Nevertheless, he was still respectful. The man was Alois' father and an important member of the community. "Please keep your money and the portrait too, Mr. Cogez. You have often been good to me." Then he called Patrasche, and the two walked home.

"We could have used the money," he murmured to Patrasche, "but I could not sell her picture."

## A CHANGE

As Mr. Cogez walked back to the mill house, he was troubled. It was against his nature to be cruel, yet he had been just that to Nello. For the moment, his social standing was more important to him than honesty to his conscience; and for the sake of his daughter and her name, he would set his true feelings aside and take other steps. "That young man must not spend so much time with Alois," he said to his wife that night. "Trouble may come out of it. He may be a nice young man, but he is poor and has no future."

"But he does have some talent," said his wife, looking admiringly at the piece of pinewood. "It really is a nice picture of Alois. I think I will hang it over the mantel beside the cuckoo clock."

"Yes, I agree," replied her husband. "I tried to give him some money for it, but he would not take it. For certain, he and the great-grandfather could have used it. I suppose he does have his pride though."

"I do not know why you are so upset about Alois spending time with Nello. You said yourself that he is a nice young man. He comes to church every Sunday. Surely that must count for something. Of course, he sits in the back. I suppose that is because he does not have nice clothes and cannot put any money in the plate when it is passed. Does that make a difference though? God says He looks on the heart. Besides, the money Alois will inherit would be enough for them to live on. Maybe he will be an artist someday."

"How can you talk so foolishly?" The miller struck the table with his fist. "That young man is nothing but a beggar, and with these painter's fancies—why, that is even worse. I am telling you, I do not want them to be together. If I have to, I will send her away to boarding school. Do you understand?"

"Yes," his surprised wife responded. She had hardly ever seen him so agitated. "Please do not send her away. I do not think I could stand that. I believe you want her here too."

Mr. Cogez said no more. In his heart, he knew he would not send Alois away, so he said no more about it or about Nello.

In the next few days, Nello and Patrasche stopped at the mill house several times, but something had changed. He did not feel welcome anymore. Alois' mother always had a job for her to do, an errand to send her on, or an appointment of some sort for her to meet. She also had studies and music lessons. Nello was a quiet but sensitive boy. He did not want to be where he was not wanted, so he stopped going to the mill house unless he had an errand there. He did not know what he had done, but he guessed he had offended Alois' father and mother by drawing the picture of Alois and Patrasche in the meadow.

Alois, on the other hand, did not know that her father had threatened to send her away to school, and she missed seeing her friend. Sometimes when she did see him, she ran up to him and took his hand and invited him to play. Nello did not tell her that he would not stay and play because he did not want her to be in trouble with her father. Not wanting to hurt her, he would say something like, "It may make your father angry. He thinks that I will keep you from your work or studies. I believe he would rather I did not come around the mill house anymore. He is a good man and dearly loves you, so we will do what pleases him, Alois."

It did not make Nello happy to say this or to stay away, but he wanted Alois to honor her parents. That would please his Heavenly Father even if it did make him sad. And it did make him very sad. The world did not seem as bright when he got up in the morning to do his work with Patrasche. The old, ruddy brown mill had been a landmark for him, and he had always looked forward to stopping by, even if just for a little while, to say hello to Alois each day. She had always watched for him and Patrasche. When they came down the little road, she would run to greet them, her blonde hair flying in the breeze. She would have a bone or a crust for Patrasche and a broad, welcoming smile for her playmate. Now, things had changed. Alois was hardly ever in the yard. Patrasche did not understand this, and he certainly missed the special treats. What neither he nor Nello knew was that Alois was often inside crying because she was not allowed to go out to meet them or be with them.

Mr. Cogez knew his decision was making Alois very unhappy, but he told himself it was best. Nello was nothing more than a beggar and was full of foolish, idle dreams. As her father, he must look to the future and what was best for his child. Her feelings were not important now. When she was older, she would understand why he had done this.

Some of the important people of the little village knew of his decision and thought he was wise. Usually that soothed his conscience, but when it bothered him too much, he would invite Nello to a party or community gathering at the mill house. In this way, Nello and Alois still saw each other once in a while, but they were not free to run and play with Patrasche as they had often done before. They were not able to talk and dream about what they wanted to do when they were adults. Alois could not make flower wreaths to hang on Patrasche's neck or watch him run across the fields with the bells on his harness jingling.

All this time, though, the little piece of pinewood still hung over the fireplace beside the cuckoo clock in the mill kitchen. This was a mystery to Alois. Why did her parents keep Nello's gift but refuse to accept him? She felt that friendship should be based on more than the work a person did or how he dressed or how much money he had.

Alois and Nello were friends because they could share things with each other—things that were important to them. If she had a problem, Nello always had a solution. Often it was a Bible verse that he shared or an illustration that the wise pastor at the old, gray church had used in some sermon. When Nello was discouraged or tired because he worked so hard, she sang hymns and happy Sunday school songs to him. Patrasche never understood all this. He just knew that Nello always whistled all the way home after he had spent time with Alois.

Now, Grandfather Jehan noticed that Nello was not as happy as he had been. He did not know why, but Nello did not want to give him any more concern, so he did not talk about what had happened at the mill house. Grandfather thought he must be sad about how hard he had to work or because he could not go to school. He said, "Yes, we are poor; yes, we work hard; but God takes care of us. We must rejoice because we have Him in our lives and a wonderful home waiting in Heaven."

Nello listened respectfully to Grandfather Jehan. He knew that what his great-grandfather said was true, and he also knew that he had given his talent and desires to the Lord. He claimed the Scriptural promise that God would give him the desires of his heart. He was the clay in the Great Potter's hand. He prayed that it would please the Potter to make him an artist. He wanted to serve God with his whole heart, and he trusted God to direct his path.

## THE BIRTHDAY PARTY

Nello's heart was broken one day when Alois came running to him in the flax fields by the canal. She had been crying. Her birthday was coming and her father was planning a big party, but Nello was not to be invited. Now that she was a little older and had asked enough questions of her mother, she knew what her father had threatened. Both she and Nello now knew why her father kept them apart. She believed her father was being very stubborn and not understanding, but Nello tried to soothe her.

"Some day it will be different, Alois," he said. "God has given me a talent, and I believe He will let me use it to serve Him. Why else would I love to draw as I do? When I am a real artist, the picture on that piece of pinewood that your father has will be worth its weight in silver. Then he will not be ashamed that I am your friend. For now, we will obey your father's wishes, but we will still be friends even if we cannot see each other very often."

What Nello said made Alois feel better. She knew he could draw beautiful pictures, but it was so hard to wait until others appreciated his artistic talent. She wondered if they ever would. He was so poor and his opportunities so few. Her father really thought he was looking out for her good. He loved her and wanted only what he thought was best for her. For now, she would be content. At least she could see Nello and Patrasche sometimes. Because Nello understood how she felt, she admired him even more. It was so special to have a friend with whom you could talk about everything—and someone who trusted God so completely. She and Nello were from very different backgrounds, but Alois felt as though he were her big brother.

"I will watch for you and Patrasche at the mill," she promised as she ran back across the field.

Nello and Patrasche went on their way too. They had work to do, and Grandfather Jehan was expecting them back before long. As they walked through the flax, Nello dreamed of the future when God would allow him to become the artist he already was in his heart. He would travel to cities in Italy and France, and then he would come back to old, familiar Flanders. Everyone would be glad to see him, especially Alois. Even her father would welcome him into their house. The piece of pinewood would not be hanging over the fireplace in the kitchen beside the cuckoo clock. It would be in a beautiful, gilded frame over the fireplace in the living room. Mr. Cogez would point it out to all his visitors and say, "The great artist Nello drew this. It is a picture of Alois when she was a little girl, and the dog was Nello's pet. Alois and Nello were always best friends." They would remember that he had once been nothing more than a beggar and would have starved had it not been for faithful Patrasche.

He stopped and patted Patrasche's heavy fur. What would he and Grandfather Jehan have done if God had not brought Patrasche to them? He fancied that someday he could buy Grandfather Jehan fine clothes to keep him warm in the cold, damp winter and that he would buy Patrasche a gold collar. Someday he would have a fine, big home by the canal. He would invite all the poor people to come to visit him. Everyone in the village would be welcome in his house. He would fix up the old, gray church too, and some of his pictures would hang on the walls inside, just as Rubens' pictures hung in the big church in Antwerp. People would come to church and hear of God's love for them, and they could freely look at his pictures. If they thanked him, he would say, "Do not thank me; thank God. He is the One Who gave me the talent and desire to paint. I just gave my life and talent to Him. He has blessed me. Do not praise me; praise Him."

His daydreams may have seemed silly, but they took Nello's mind away from thoughts of Alois. On the day of her birthday, he was happy for his friend. He and Patrasche, of course, could not go to her party. Instead, they went home by themselves to the little dark hut and a meal of black bread. In the mill house, all the other children of the village sang and laughed and ate and played games. Nello wanted to give Alois a birthday present, but he could not. The only thing he could do was pray that she would continue to honor her father's wishes until God changed the man's heart.

"Never mind, Patrasche," he said as he sat with his arms around the big dog's neck. From the door of the hut, they could hear the sounds of the party carried on the breeze from the village. "God knows about this, and someday it will be different. God will change Mr. Cogez's heart. Until then, we must wait patiently."

"This is Alois' birthday, isn't it?" asked Grandfather Jehan. The old man was stretched out on his hard bed in a dark corner of the hut.

Nello nodded in assent. He had hoped his great-grandfather would not remember so he would not have to explain.

"Why aren't you there, Nello? You have always gone to her birthday parties. I hope nothing has happened between you."

"I decided to stay with you." It was true he had decided to stay with his great-grandfather; but what else could he do, since he had not been invited to the party?

"I could have stayed by myself. I stay by myself often. I think there is more to this," he insisted. "You did not have cross words with Alois, did you?"

How could he keep back the truth from his great-grandfather? "No, Grandfather Jehan. I would never argue with Alois. If you must know the real reason, I was not invited. Her father does not want us to spend time together."

"You have not done anything wrong, have you?" questioned Grandfather Jehan.

"Nothing," replied Nello. "I just drew a picture of Alois and Patrasche on a piece of pine. That is all."

"Ah!" The old man was silent. He understood the truth. He might be sick and bedridden most of the time, but he was not blind or ignorant to what went on in the village. He pulled Nello's curly blond head to his chest. "You are poor, my child," he said, his voice quavering. "You are so poor, and I know how hard it is for you because of it."

"But I am rich, Grandfather Jehan. I do not have a nice house or nice clothes. I do not know how to read or write, but I am rich. I have you and Patrasche, and I am God's child." To himself he thought, "God has blessed me with a special talent, and someday Mr. Cogez will not be ashamed for me to visit his house."

He went and stood by the door of the hut in the quiet autumn night and watched the stars troop by and the tall poplars bend and shiver in the wind. He could see all the bright lights shining from the mill house. He could hear

the merry laughter of children's voices. He believed what he had told Grandfather Jehan; still, that did not make it any easier. Tears fell down his cheeks because it hurt to be left out. He stayed there, looking toward the village and listening until all was quiet and dark. Then he and Patrasche went inside and slept.

## THE SECRET

Nello had one secret that only Patrasche knew. There was a little shed behind their hut, which no one entered but the two of them. Though the shed was a rather dreary place, great light poured in through the windows on the north side. In this shed, Nello had made a crude easel out of rough lumber. There, on a large sheet of gray paper, he had drawn one of the many pictures he fancied in his brain. No one had ever taught him anything about art. He had no money to buy paints, and he had gone without bread many times to get the rough boards for the easel and a few other drawing supplies. Without paints, he could only draw in black and white. The eye-catching figure he had captured in charcoal on the gray paper was an old man sitting on a fallen tree.

Nello had seen old Michel the woodsman sitting that way many times in the evening. No one had taught Nello about outline or perspective, about anatomy or shadow; and yet he had given his picture all the weary, worn-out aging, all the sad, quiet patience, all the rugged, careworn emotions of the old woodsman. It was beautiful in its simplicity and feeling. The figure was like a poem. The old woodsman sat meditative and alone on the dead tree, with the darkness of the descending night behind him. The picture was rough and the style untaught, of course. It had artistic flaws, no doubt; yet it was lifelike, true in nature, true in art, and very beautiful.

Patrasche lay quietly for countless hours watching the gradual creation of the masterpiece after his and Nello's work was done each day. Nello had a hope—wild and foolish perhaps, but bold. He hoped to enter the drawing in a contest. The prize for the winner was two hundred francs a year. He had heard about the contest in Antwerp; and it was open to any talented young person, wealthy or peasant, under eighteen, who entered a work in chalk or charcoal. Three of the most respected artists from the town where Rubens had once worked were to be the judges. They would select the most deserving winner—the one who showed the most promise as an artist.

All spring, summer, and autumn, Nello worked on his treasure. The contest, if he won, would be his first step toward independence and his goal of becoming a great artist. That goal to fulfill his God-given gift would be his avenue of service for his Lord. It was not just for himself that he wanted to win. Winning would bring glory to God and would provide a way for him to take care of Grandfather Jehan.

Nello did not tell Grandfather Jehan his plans or show him the drawing. His great-grandfather would not have

understood. Alois would have understood and would have been excited and full of hope for him, but he was not able to share his hope with her. The only one who knew was Patrasche. To Patrasche he whispered, "I am praying that I may be an artist for His glory alone. God has done so much for me, and I want to be all I can be for Him."

Patrasche did not understand because he was a dog. Had he understood, he would have known that everything Nello did was under the Saviour's ever watchful eye. It was He Who had given Nello his artistic talent, and He was pleased that Nello wanted to use that talent for Him. Nello was just a boy of fifteen, but he was far wiser in character than many grown men.

All drawings were to be entered on the first day of December, and the winner would be announced on the twenty-fourth, the day before Christmas. For the winner, the prize would be a wonderful Christmas present. And so, on the evening before the entries had to be in, Nello carefully wrapped his picture and put it on the old green milk cart and set off for Antwerp. His stomach churned with anticipation. He knew his picture was good, but would the judges think it the best? Much hard work and prayer had gone into his masterpiece. However, many other young contestants were also hopeful. Although they looked forward to the honor and prestige the award would bring them, those were not the reasons Nello wanted to win. He, Grandfather Jehan, and Patrasche needed the money. The hut needed repairs, Grandfather needed medicine, Nello needed a new jacket, and more nourishing food would be a blessing too. These were reasons enough for Nello's winning, but there was an even more important reason. If he won, he would know that God wanted him to be an artist as much as he wanted to be one.

It was nearly dark when Patrasche and Nello reached the closed doors of the large public building in Antwerp. The only thing to do was to leave the drawing on the steps so that the judges would find it in the morning. "Maybe the judges will not like it at all," Nello began to doubt. "It is a rather sad picture. Perhaps I should have drawn a happy scene with children playing. No, no, this is the picture I had to draw," he finally convinced himself, "but they will never give the prize to someone poor and ignorant like me. Look, my toes are sticking out of my stockings, my coat is patched, and I cannot read or write. What chance do I have?" Then he remembered that it was not chance that would decide if he would win. It was in God's hands.

As he and Patrasche trudged home, his stomach no longer churned. He had done his best, and the rest must be as God willed. No matter how the contest turned out, he would thank God. It was a cold night, but when they passed the old, gray church in the center of his village, Nello felt a warmness in his heart greater than the hearth fire in the mill house that stood on the opposite side of the lane. God's love and peace were eternal; wealth was not.

After they reached the hut, snow began to fall. It fell all night and for several days after that. The cold was bitter and the wind blew sharply, finding its way through the cracks in the walls of the hut. The canal and all the streams were frozen over, and the roads and paths were obliterated.

Nevertheless, the milk had to go to town. It was hard work for Nello and Patrasche to go from house to house and then to Antwerp in the blinding snow and cold. Nello did not have proper clothing for such weather, and pulling the cart in the deep snow was hard work for Patrasche. He was getting old and his joints were stiff and his bones ached in the bitter cold, but he faithfully plodded ahead.

Seeing how hard it was for Patrasche, Nello thought he would rather be doing the work himself, but each morning the big dog was ready and willing to go. The only thing Patrasche had ever known was being in a harness. Work was his life. He suffered from the cold, and he had a great deal of pain in his limbs; but he pulled hard and never let his master down, even though Nello sometimes had to push the cart from behind when it got stuck in a rut or drift.

Sometimes Nello would say, "Stay at home with Grandfather today, Patrasche. I can pull the cart myself."

Even Grandfather Jehan would urge Patrasche to remain in the hut with him. "We are both very old. Stay here with me today and keep me company." Grandfather would reach out and stroke the big dog on his head, but Patrasche would not stay behind.

If a dog could reason, he probably would have thought, "I must work faithfully until I die." Sometimes it seemed that time was not far away. Not only did his joints and bones stiffen and ache, but he was also losing his sight. Still, every morning at five o'clock when the bell from the old, gray church rang out across the fields, Patrasche was up, ready to go with Nello. He never shirked but, like a tired soldier, did his duty. The cart was there to pull, and he pulled it—over the snow and through the fields—just as he had pulled it for so many years.

Each time Patrasche and Nello left to take the milk, Grandfather would lie back on his bed and wonder, "What will become of Nello after Patrasche and I are gone?"

## TRAGEDY AT THE MILL

One afternoon, as the two of them came back from Antwerp over the snow, which had become hard and smooth as marble on the fields, they found a little puppet, a tambourine player, painted scarlet and gold, and about six inches (15 cm) high. Nello assumed that some Christmas shopper had probably dropped it. He tried to find out from a shopkeeper to whom it belonged so he could return it, but no one claimed it. Finally the shopkeeper said, "No one has come back for it. Perhaps they do not even live around here. It was paid for, so it is yours. Give it to someone as a Christmas gift."

Nello was hesitant to keep it but finally decided that perhaps God had brought it his way so he could give a present to Alois. She would be pleased with it.

It was quite dark when he passed the mill house, but he knew where Alois' bedroom window was. Surely it would not hurt to stop just this once. Then she would know that he still wanted to be her friend.

There was a little shed with a sloping roof attached to the house. He climbed up and tapped on her window. He could see a light inside, and in a moment Alois appeared. When she saw him, there was a puzzled look on her face, but she opened the window.

Nello handed the little tambourine player to her and said, "Here is a puppet for you, Alois. I found it in the snow. I think maybe God put it there so I would have a present to give to you for Christmas. Take it and God bless you."

Before she had time to thank him, he slid down from the shed roof and ran off through the darkness. It would have been wonderful to have stayed to talk with her, but he could not chance being caught by Mr. Cogez. Most of all, he did not want Alois to be in trouble with her father. However, as he ran, he glanced back to see Mr. Cogez looking out a lower-floor window.

That night there was a fire at the mill. The fire destroyed several buildings and much flax, although the mill itself and the house where the family lived were not damaged. The whole village was in an uproar and came out to see what was happening. The miller, Alois' father, had insurance so his buildings could be replaced, but he was furious and insisted that the fire was not an accident— someone had set it. He had enemies because he was not always an easy businessman with whom to deal. Quite naturally, he assumed someone was getting even for some unhappy business deal.

The next morning, there was still much commotion at the mill. When Nello heard about the fire, he rushed to the

mill to see if anyone had been hurt. Mr. Cogez saw him and grabbed him angrily. "So now you show up! You were here after dark and up to no good! I think you know more about this fire than anyone." Mr. Cogez knew that Nello had seen Alois last night, and now he accused him of starting the fire.

Nello was shocked. At first he thought Mr. Cogez must be joking, but he quickly realized the man was serious. The miller's words stung Nello's ears. Yes, he had been there last night. He could not deny that, but he certainly had nothing to do with setting the fire. Why would he want to endanger Alois' life?

Mr. Cogez did not press charges against Nello. Apparently, after thinking about his rash statements, he realized how foolish they had been. He had been very upset and wanted someone to blame for the fire. However, he had accused Nello publicly and then continued his accusations to neighbors and townspeople who came by the mill.

This was a cruel thing to do, because soon word was out that Nello had been snooping around the mill the night of the fire. Mr. Cogez even said Nello held a grudge against him because he would not let the boy come to the mill house anymore. Deep inside, Mr. Cogez knew none of this was true. In fact, his conscience greatly bothered him over the way he had been treating Nello. He knew it was not right, but he did nothing to call back his angry words or try to make amends with Nello.

Sadly, because the people of the village wanted to remain on good terms with the richest man in town, they not only listened but also began to shun Nello. Wherever Nello went, people gave him suspicious looks and turned their backs on him. They said nothing to him openly, but shopkeepers and neighbors avoided him. Worst of all, at some of the farms where Nello and Patrasche went to pick up the daily milk supply, they received downcast glances and mumbled greetings. Where before they had been warmly received with broad smiles and kind words, they now got hardly a glance or short word in greeting.

Not many people really believed what the miller had said, but they preferred to have him as their friend rather than Nello. They were ignorant people who had forgotten what their dusty Bibles said about how to treat the poor. They thought only of themselves and their comforts. Nello did not try to defend himself. Even if he had, they would not have listened to him, for their minds were made up. It was better to stay on the good side of the miller, they had decided. Why should they bother themselves about Nello, his ailing great-grandfather, and his poor aging dog of Flanders?

There were a few people in the village who did not listen to the miller because they pitied Grandfather, Nello, and Patrasche. However, Nello did not want their pity; he wanted their respect. He wanted them to believe that he would never do something so wrong as setting a fire.

One day Alois' mother went to her husband. She was nearly in tears. "You used to be a kind, generous man, but now you have become a hard man. The way you are treating Nello is not right, and what you say about him to the townspeople is not true. You know as well as I do that he had nothing to do with the fire at the mill. You only contrived that to hurt him because you do not want him to see or visit Alois. How can you be so cruel? It is hurting our little Alois and me as much as it is hurting Nello. Nello is a good, honest, hardworking young man. You should be glad your daughter picks such friends."

Mr. Cogez was too stubborn and proud to admit that his wife was right. He did not like himself for the accusations he had made, but he did not have enough courage or humility to admit he was wrong. He had forgotten that "Pride goeth before destruction, and an haughty spirit before a fall."

# HOMEGOING

Nello patiently endured the injury done against him, comforting himself in the knowledge that he was innocent of any wrongdoing and had nothing to do with the fire. He had another comfort, too, that he shared only with Patrasche. "If I win the contest, things will be different. I will not be so poor, and Mr. Cogez will not be ashamed to have me around. That will set things right. Now I have another reason to win!"

Despite the weather and unkind treatment from the villagers, Nello and Patrasche faithfully continued to take what milk was still entrusted to them to Antwerp each day. Nevertheless, it was a difficult time. Until the fire, he had been treated kindly at least, and on occasion he had even received special favors. Now the contrast seemed all the harsher. He felt as if the whole world were against him— all the world except Patrasche. Of course, Grandfather Jehan also loved him. He knew that, but Grandfather did not know what had happened, and Nello was not about to cause him any worry by telling him.

Even the bitter cold weather seemed against them. Neighbors sat beside their blazing fires and either had no idea or did not care about how miserable it was in the little hut on the edge of town. They talked with each other, visited each other, and prepared for a merry Christmas season; but Nello and Patrasche were not invited to their celebrations. Instead, they were left to care for the old, paralyzed, bedridden great-grandfather in their bleak, drafty room, where the fire burned low and sometimes there was nothing to eat.

Eventually most of the uncaring farmers started sending their milk with another carrier. He had a mule instead of a dog, and he could carry more. Only three or four people refused the new man's terms and remained faithful to the little green cart. So, the load Patrasche pulled each day grew lighter, while the burden in Nello's heart grew heavier every day and the coins in his pocket became fewer.

Patrasche did not understand any of this. Each day he dragged himself to his harness and stopped at each familiar gate and looked toward the door as if waiting for someone to come out. To many of the neighbors, it was sad and painful. They would peek from behind their curtains and sometimes wipe a tear until Patrasche gave up and pulled the cart to another door. Later, they would question why they had been so cruel. Now, however, pride swelled up in them. They wanted man's approval more than God's.

Christmas was just a few days off. The weather had not let up one bit, and it was still windy and cold. The snow was six feet (2 m) deep, and the ice in the canal was thick enough to bear the weight of horses and wagons. However, not even the weather stopped the holiday spirit. During this season, the little village was always gay and cheerful with decorations and happy, excited children. Merriment was all around. Even the horses had jingling bells on their harnesses.

In even the poorest homes, there were cookies and cakes, puddings and pies, and little presents in bright paper and ribbons. Greenery decorated the doorways and staircases. Good smells floated out of every kitchen. Geese were ready for roasting. Everyone wore festive holiday dress, and relatives were coming from far and near to be with their families.

No one was alone . . . except in the dreary, dark, cold hut on the edge of town. Nello and Patrasche were now utterly alone; for, two days before Christmas, Death had visited and had taken away Grandfather Jehan. His visit was not unexpected, but it certainly was not welcome.

For some time, the old soldier had been too weak to get up and move about. He could not even speak. Nello had tried to get some warm broth down his throat, but he was too weak to swallow it or the stale bread dipped in it. He gently went in his sleep, without a murmur or complaint, to be with his Heavenly Father. He had been longing to be with his Saviour. He had only clung to this world because of Nello. Now the struggle was over, and he was home safe in the arms of Jesus.

Nello had comfort knowing that his great-grandfather was in Heaven, but still he grieved deeply. For some time after finding the cold, stiff body of the only man who had truly loved him, he sat sobbing. All this was a mystery to Patrasche. He did not understand why Nello was crying, and always before, if Nello did cry for some reason—a cut or bruise—Grandfather Jehan always spoke soothing words. He had been just a poor, feeble, paralyzed old man who could not raise a hand in their defense; yet he had loved them. His welcome smile had greeted them at the end of each hard day.

Finally, Nello went for the pastor at the little, gray church. The pastor was not at all surprised at the news Nello brought, but he was sad that it had happened during the holiday season. Death always seemed sadder then, even though it was never really sad for a child of God to go to Heaven. Nello knew this, but he also knew that the one person who had always loved and cared for him was now gone, and he and Patrasche were left totally alone.

Somehow the pastor found a suitable crate to use for a casket. Only Nello and Patrasche were at the unmarked grave when the pastor read the Scripture about "from dust to dust."

After the brief service, the pastor took them home for a warm supper, but neither of them could eat much. The pastor tried to encourage them, but he was very poor also. At this time of year, he tried to help where it was most needed, but he had little to give. Offerings were small, especially at Christmas, because people felt obligated to buy gifts for family before they put anything in the offering plate. More often than not, there was nothing left to give after gifts were bought. Before nightfall, the pastor's wife tucked a little food under Nello's arm, and he and Patrasche went home to the empty hut. It was cold and dark. Though it was not much, it was their home.

## OUT IN THE COLD

When Alois' mother heard that Nello's great-grandfather had passed away, she wanted to go to comfort him, or at least send some food to the little hut. Nevertheless, she knew she dared not cross her husband's wishes. "Surely now, once he thinks about it, he will change his mind about Nello. Perhaps he will let him come and visit Alois. What can it hurt? The boy is all alone and needs someone to care for him."

Mr. Cogez suspected what she was thinking. "The boy is nothing but a beggar. I do not want him around our child," he declared. He had hardened his heart and would not allow himself to think about it and would not even let his wife talk about it. Later, Mrs. Cogez sent flowers for the unmarked grave.

Nello and Patrasche had each other. Somehow they would have to make it alone. "Thankfully, we have a place to live. It is not much; but, if we can survive the winter, I will find another job in the spring and we will fix up the hut. That is what Grandfather Jehan would want us to do."

The sad truth was that, for all the years Grandfather Jehan had lived in the hut, he did not own it. It was rented, and when the great-grandfather died, the rent for that month was already overdue. When the landlord came to collect his rent, Nello had nothing to give him. He had given the minister a coin for the funeral and bought some dark bread. Then everything was gone. He begged the landlord to show some mercy and give him time to earn the few coins. The man was a cobbler and he had plenty of coins. He went to church every Sunday in Antwerp. Surely he could wait a few days.

The cobbler was also a good friend of the miller, Mr. Cogez; and, like the miller, wealth was very important to him. Instead of showing mercy, he harshly told Nello that he must move out the next day. Because of the overdue rent, everything in the hut now belonged to him, including the little green cart and the harness. If Nello did not get out, he would send someone to throw him out. The only thing Nello could take with him were his Bible and the shabby clothes he was wearing.

What more could happen? Nello and Patrasche had been unjustly accused and unfairly treated by their neighbors. They had lost the only person in the world who really loved them, and now they were being put out of the dilapidated hut that was their home. They had no place to go, no person to help them, and no means of livelihood.

As they huddled together in the dark, cold hut, they forgot how truly miserable it was. All they knew was that it was home. They had been happy there. In the summer, with its climbing vines and blossoms, it was a bright spot in the middle of the sunlit fields. Yes, they had worked hard and had little, but they were content. After every long, hard day, they could run here and find Great-grandfather with open arms and heart. His smiles of love and welcome never failed. Now, how very lonely they were. Even God seemed to have left them.

All night long, Nello and Patrasche sat in the dark hut. They had no fire to keep them warm, so they snuggled close to each other. Their bodies were cold and their hearts seemed frozen with sorrow. To Nello, even the possibility of winning the art contest provided very little encouragement.

In the morning, the dawn broke over a white, cold landscape. It was the day before Christmas. There was merriment and the joy of anticipation in the village, but Nello and Patrasche were homeless. Nello hugged his only friend as hot tears rolled down his cheeks and fell onto Patrasche's broad forehead. "We have to go, Patrasche. We will not wait until the cobbler comes to throw us out. We will leave now."

Patrasche did as he always did and obeyed his master. Side by side they left the little hut, the only home they had ever known. It was just a hovel, but still it held all the memories of love and comfort that either of them had ever known.

As they passed the little green cart, Patrasche hesitated a bit, dropped his head wearily, but then followed Nello. He could no longer pull it. The cart now belonged to the cobbler. The harness, too, with its tiny bells, lay in the snow. The big dog did not understand why Nello did not stop and put it on him. However, he faithfully followed close to the boy who loved him and needed him.

The two of them walked the same road they had always traveled to Antwerp, but this time there was no little green cart with brass cans of milk. As they passed the houses, most blinds were still closed. It was barely past daylight and most villagers were just getting dressed and having breakfast. No one saw the boy and his dog as they trudged by. Once Nello stopped in front of a house. He decided to go up and knock. His great-grandfather had often shown kindness to these people. Surely they would show kindness to him in return.

"Do you have any scraps for Patrasche?" he asked timidly. "He is old and has not had anything to eat since yesterday morning."

As the woman slammed the door in his face, she mumbled something about food being too expensive to waste on a dog. The two of them went on. Their stomachs were empty, but they did not ask for help again. The cold made Patrasche's joints stiff and painful. The chilling air went right through Nello's thin jacket and froze his bare fingers that stuck out from the old, worn-out gloves. Antwerp seemed much farther away today, but they finally reached the town square as the chimes in the great church rang ten.

"If I had anything I could sell to buy Patrasche some bread, I would do it," thought Nello. He did not have a thing, though, except his Bible, his thin jacket, and his wooden shoes.

Patrasche understood and nestled his nose into Nello's hand as if to say, "I understand, master. Do not worry about me. I am old and have seen harder times than these."

They had come to Antwerp, of course, for a very special reason. The winner of the art contest would be announced at noon today. There was still hope. If his drawing were selected, Nello would have enough money not only to pay the rent but also to buy the little hut. He could buy food for both himself and Patrasche, and he could get a warmer coat and gloves. It would not matter about a cart. They would not need it, for people would pay Nello to paint pictures for them. Nello and Patrasche would not be rich, not really, only rich in comparison to what they had now. They would be taken care of, and "having food and raiment," they would be content. Oh, surely this was how

God would work it all out! But Nello could not demand this of God. "For Your honor, Father. Whatever will bring the most honor to You," Nello prayed, and in his heart he did so hope this was the way.

Nello and Patrasche tramped a little farther to the public building where they had left his treasured masterpiece days before. The steps and entrance were crowded with people. Nello saw several boys his own age, though some were older. Parents, relatives, and friends were there too, for this was an important day. Among this group might be another Rubens. In their anticipation, no one seemed to notice the poorly dressed boy and the big, weary dog standing in a corner of the hall. Nello pulled Patrasche close to him.

Then the door to the auditorium opened and everyone rushed in. At the same time, all the bells in the city churches announced the noon hour. The excitement was almost too much for Nello, or was it the lack of food that made his head swim? His vision blurred for a moment. He thought he would faint.

Everyone knew the winning picture would be displayed on a large easel on the platform. There was the easel and a picture. His head and vision cleared a little. Was it? Was it? It was not! Then the blood drained from his head and he slumped to the floor in utter disappointment. Through what seemed a mist, Nello heard the announcement that the prize had gone to Stephen Kiesslinger, who lived in Antwerp. He was the son of a shipyard worker at the harbor.

Weakly, Nello picked himself up and wandered outside into the chilly air. Despair overwhelmed him. What disappointed him more about not winning? Was it that he did not know how he and Patrasche would survive now, or was it that he had needed this sign to know God wanted him to be an artist? He looked heavenward as if looking for another sign, but there was none. In the distance, he saw the winner surrounded by friends and family. They were applauding and congratulating him. It did not seem fair, but God had never promised that this world would be fair to His children. Did anyone need the prize more than Nello and Patrasche? However, it was not a matter of need; it was a matter of God's will.

Nello knelt down and pulled Patrasche into his arms. For what seemed a long time, he buried his head in the big dog's fur and sobbed. Disappointment totally overcame him. "It is all over, dear Patrasche," he murmured. "All over."

Finally, he got up. He was weak from not eating and overwhelmed with disappointment. Together he and Patrasche retraced their steps to the village. There was only one place he felt he could go and find comfort.

## THE MIRACLE

The snow was falling quickly and a sharp north wind was blowing. It was bitterly cold. It took Nello and Patrasche a long time to reach the village, even though the way was so familiar. The bell in the old, gray church was chiming four o'clock when Patrasche suddenly paused. Something in the snow had caught his attention. He sniffed at something under the new-fallen snow, scratched, and whined. Then with his teeth he pulled out a small, brown leather wallet and held it up to Nello. They were near light from a nearby house, so Nello turned the wallet toward the light to see if he could find any identification. He did not have to look inside, however, because engraved on the outside in gold was the name B. Cogez. Nello could not help but notice that the wallet was stuffed with bills. He guessed there must be at least two thousand francs.

Finding the wallet was a shock that awakened all Nello's senses. Blood rushed to his face. His feet and hands tingled. Was this a miracle? Had God given him this money? Did Mr. Cogez even know he had lost it? More questions came, and the temptation to keep the wallet and the money crossed his mind. He was hungry and cold, and Patrasche was too. They needed this provision, but would it be honest? Mr. Cogez had treated them very unfairly, and here was an opportunity to pay him back. However, one powerful thought pushed away all others. ". . . do good to them that hate you . . . ." Nello tucked the wallet under his jacket, patted Patrasche, and pulled him forward. The dog looked up hopefully at Nello. He was only a dog, but he knew that wallets got food. Would they go to the market now?

Nello walked straight to the mill house. He was determined to do what he must do. He went to the door and knocked. The miller's wife opened it. She had been crying. Alois was behind her with wide eyes, watching carefully.

"Oh, it's you, Nello," Mrs. Cogez said kindly. "Go away before Mr. Cogez sees you here. We have trouble tonight. Right now Mr. Cogez is out in this storm looking for a lot of money that he lost while riding home. He dropped his wallet somewhere and will have an impossible job finding it in this snow. If he does not find it, we will be ruined. It was all our savings. Why he had it out in the snow, I will never know. This must surely be God's judgment on us for treating you so badly."

Nello stepped inside for a moment and put the wallet in her hand. Then he called Patrasche inside also. The old dog was grateful for the warmth. "Tell Mr. Cogez that Patrasche found the wallet tonight," Nello said quietly. "If you do, I think he will give Patrasche shelter and food in his old age. Do not let Patrasche follow me, and be good to him."

Before either Mrs. Cogez or Patrasche realized what he meant, Nello stooped and kissed Patrasche. Then he closed the door hurriedly and disappeared back into the snowy night.

Mrs. Cogez and Alois stood speechless. What had happened seemed unbelievable. Had Patrasche really found the wallet? If so, where? Why would anyone expect Nello to return it to Mr. Cogez after the miller had blamed him for setting the mill fire?

As they stood staring, Patrasche went to the door and tried to follow his master. He barked, something he hardly ever did, and he ran against the door. The girl and her mother did not dare open it and let him out; Nello had made it clear he did not want Patrasche to follow him. They tried everything to calm the animal down. They brought a bowl of water and a piece of lean meat. They offered him everything they could think of that might be a treat for a dog. He was wet and shivering from being out in the cold and from fear. They tried to dry him off and get him to lie down by the fire, but he would not. He refused to be comforted or to move from the door, where he stood whining.

### *ALL IS FORGIVEN*

It was five o'clock when the miller finally came in the back door. His face was red from the cold, and his eyes showed his despair. He was a broken man. "It is lost forever," he said with a quiver in his stern voice. "We have looked with lanterns everywhere. It is gone—all that we had saved and all we had set aside for Alois' education. All of it!"

His wife put the brown wallet into his hand. He stared at it with open mouth. He could not say a word; he was too stunned. First, he had lost the money, then he had lost hope, and now both had been given back. What did it all mean? Then she told him how it had been returned. The strong man sank trembling into a chair and covered his face with his hands. He was ashamed and, at the same time, afraid. Was this God's judgment? "I have been so cruel to the boy," he muttered finally. "I certainly do not deserve any good from him. He is more of a man than I am."

Alois, who loved her father dearly, also loved her friend Nello and took this opportunity to be courageous. "Father, does this mean Nello may come here again?" she asked. "May he come tomorrow for Christmas dinner?"

The miller took her in his strong arms. His hard face had softened, and his voice trembled. "Certainly, certainly! He may come on Christmas Day and any other day he wants to come," he said. "God helping me, I will make amends to him for all I have done. I have been a selfish, cruel man. I see it now. I am not pleased with myself, and I know God is not pleased with my actions. I will try to make it up to Nello. You will see that I mean it."

Alois hugged and kissed her father in gratitude and joy. It was the best Christmas present she could have gotten. Then she ran to Patrasche who was still waiting for the door to open so he could go find his master. "Father, may we keep Patrasche here and feed him tonight?" she pleaded happily.

Again her father hung his head shamefully, for he had been mean to the dog as well. "Of course. Let him stay and give him the very best."

This was quite a change. Tragedy had threatened the miller where it hurt the most—in his bank account. How remorseful and yet how grateful he was when he realized how little his money really mattered in comparison with love from family and compassion from friends. He did not deserve God's goodness, and he had finally come to realize it when it was almost too late. God could have taken everything he owned and loved. He could have taken his wife and young daughter. Yes, God has ways of getting the attention of His children when they disobey Him. Mr. Cogez saw how wrong he had been. His heart was touched, and he was truly sorry for the pain he had caused Nello and his family. Now he had another chance, and he would make amends if only God were to give him opportunity.

It was Christmas Eve, and the mill house showed it from every mantel and corner. Stacks of oak logs burned in every fireplace; plates of cookies and pots of steaming hot cocoa sat waiting to be sampled. A large tree was trimmed with holly berries and tinsel. Boughs of holly and evergreen were draped across the ceiling rafters and doorways. Very large wreaths hung on the front door and over the main fireplace in the parlor. A smaller wreath hung over the kitchen fireplace next to the cuckoo clock and the picture Nello had drawn of Alois and Patrasche. Candles burned, puddings bubbled, and warmth and abundance filled every room.

Alois was overjoyed with the presence of Patrasche and showered on him all the attention a dog could desire, but he would not come close to the warm fire or eat the tasty morsels set before him. He was cold and hungry; but, without his beloved master, he would not accept the comfort or satisfaction offered by Alois and her parents. They tried every way they knew to get him to eat, but he would not. Instead, he posted himself at the door, watching for a way to escape.

"He wants the lad," said Mr. Cogez. "Good dog! Good dog! I will go get him first thing in the morning."

No one but Patrasche knew Nello was not at the hut or that the selfish cobbler had driven them out. How could they have guessed that at that very moment Nello was facing starvation and misery from the cold? Only Patrasche knew.

The mill kitchen was very warm. Great logs crackled and flamed on the hearth. Neighbors came in for a cup of cocoa. They sampled the holiday treats and the roast goose that had been baked for supper. Alois was happier than she had been in months. Tomorrow she would have her playmate back. She twirled around the room, clapping her hands and tossing her blonde curls over her shoulders. Mr. Cogez's heart rejoiced to see her this way again after months of forlorn, low spirits. Joyful tears moistened his eyes as much over her change as over his own change of heart. For months it had felt as if a tight band were around his chest. Now it was gone, and he felt as though he would burst with new freedom. He continually spoke of Nello and the things he would do for the orphan the next day and all the days ahead. He would welcome him at the mill house again, and Nello and dear Alois would be the best of friends again.

Mrs. Cogez sat in her favorite chair near the warmth of the fireplace. Her face was again content as she worked on some needlepoint, greeted neighbors, and sipped hot cocoa. The lines and wrinkles of concern had melted away with the change in her husband. The cuckoo clock chirped away the hours. The household was blessed, comfortable, and content.

In the middle of all this was Patrasche. They coaxed him repeatedly to leave his post at the door and eat or lie by the fire. None of this tempted him. Too many days the sun of Nello's love had warmed him. Too many hours they had trudged along together with the little green cart.

Later, amid the happy voices and coming and going of guests, Patrasche found the opportunity he had been awaiting; he slipped out the door as some careless guests came in. As swiftly as his weak, stiff, tired legs would carry him, he trotted over the snow in the bitter black night. He had only one thought—to find Nello. A human friend might have eaten or slept first, but that was not the kind of friendship Nello and Patrasche had. All he remembered was that, in some long-ago past, an old man and a little child had found him near death by the side of the road.

## A COLD NIGHT

It was nearly eleven o'clock, and more snow was falling. The trail of Nello's wooden shoes had been blotted out, and even his scent was not easy to find. After Patrasche found it one time, he lost it; then he found it again.

The wind howled, drifts grew against the doors and curbs, and the roads were sheets of ice. The few street lamps had been blown out by the wind. All the cattle were in the barns, and warmth seemed to glow at the windows of even the humblest little cottage or hut as Christmas Day approached. Warmth was inside, but Patrasche—old, famished, cold, and full of pain—was outside in the cruel cold. Nevertheless, love urged him on. He was determined to find Nello.

The trail of Nello's steps, faint and obscure under the new snow, went straight across the village street to the old, gray church. Had he been able to reason like a human, Patrasche would have realized that Nello would most certainly go to the place that was almost as dear to him as the old hut. The church was not far from the mill house, but because so many guests and travelers had gone up and down the street and sidewalks, it took Patrasche some time to follow his master's trail to the steps of the old, gray church. The doors of the old church were never locked.

Patrasche had always been left outside when Nello came to church. He did not understand why he could not go into this building, but when his master made a request, he obeyed. Besides, it was not an unpleasant wait. He could hear singing and the sonorous voice of the pastor. There was a certain stern pleading, yet loving welcome, in the tone of that voice. Nello and Patrasche had been to the pastor's home, and there Patrasche was allowed in the kitchen. It was a warm and welcome place.

Tonight was different, though. The old dog must find his master. He nudged one side of the double door, and it quietly opened just a little. Patrasche pushed through. Inside it was dark and nearly as cold as the outside, but at least he was out of the wind and falling snow. The fire in the stove that warmed the room had gone out long before, and the pastor had gone home to be with his family. In the dim light, Patrasche could hardly see the white tracks of snow left by Nello's wooden shoes. He followed them to the front and there, stretched out on the kneeling bench, was Nello. Patrasche lightly padded to the boy and touched his nose against Nello's cheek as if to say, "Why did you leave me? Did you think I would not be faithful always? Have I done wrong in seeking to find you?"

When Nello's cold hand reached out to him, a little murmur escaped the boy's lips. He drew the big, old dog

close to him. "No one on this earth cares about us," he sobbed to Patrasche. "I did not know where else to go. I do not want to bother the pastor's family and spoil their Christmas Eve."

In truth, the pastor would have welcomed Nello and Patrasche had he known of their situation, but the cobbler, who had driven them from their home, had kept his cruel deed secret. Men do all kinds of heartless acts because of their greed and love of money.

Patrasche nuzzled as close to Nello as possible. He was content to be near his master again.

The blasts that blew over the Flemish dikes and canals from the North Sea that night were like waves of ice that froze every living thing they touched. In the cold church, Nello and Patrasche fell asleep. Together they dreamed of the happy days when they had chased each other through the flowering grasses of the summer meadows or hidden in the tall bulrushes by the water's side to watch the boats go seaward in the sun. They also remembered the day in the meadow behind the mill when Alois had made flower chains for their necks and Nello had drawn the picture of Alois and Patrasche on the piece of pine. "Oh, God, how I wanted to be an artist for You," Nello whispered in his dream. "I wanted to use my gift to serve and honor You."

The next morning dawned clear and full of sunshine as it often does after a terrific winter storm. As he had promised, Mr. Cogez went to find Nello and Patrasche at the hut. When he did not find them, he returned to town. Since the hut belonged to his friend, the cobbler, the miller stopped there to ask if he knew anything about the boy and his dog. When the cobbler reported that he had taken back his property and turned them out, Mr. Cogez was horrified. "You turned them out in this cold? Why didn't you say something to me? I would have taken them in."

"You would have taken them into your house? Never!" reminded the cobbler. "Have you forgotten all the rumors you have spread about the boy? I do not know where the two of them have gone, but I certainly thought you, of all people, would approve of my collecting what was mine."

The miller was nearly frantic. Where would a homeless boy and dog have found refuge on Christmas Eve in such a storm? "The church, of course!" he shouted, suddenly full of inspiration. "Perhaps he went to the church. No doubt he spent the night at the parsonage."

He hurried down the village lanes to the old, gray church. As he approached, he noticed faint dog tracks—those of a big, heavy dog—leading to the front door. At least Patrasche had been there. As Mr. Cogez entered, the pastor met him. He was struck by the sadness on the pastor's face. The miller was nearly frantic as the minister pointed with outstretched arm toward the front and continued shaking his head.

By now bright sunshine was beaming through the old stained-glass windows. Light covered the scene, and there, with his head on the shaggy fur of his faithful companion, was Nello. A blanket covered both of them.

Mr. Cogez noticed that a fire burned in the stove, but the two figures were not moving. He immediately believed they were both dead—that they had come to the church the night before and the bitter cold had claimed them. His jaw dropped helplessly.

Before Mr. Cogez could say anything, the pastor spoke quietly. "It is so sad," he said, shaking his head again. "I suppose his grief and loneliness after losing his great-grandfather was too unbearable in the old hut. The two of them evidently came here to get out of the cold. If they had only come around to the parsonage, my wife and I would have gladly given them a warm place to sleep."

"No, pastor, it is not your fault." Mr. Cogez looked at the two still bodies, lying motionless at the front. His voice grew hoarse and louder. "It seems the cobbler put the boy and his dog out of their hut. Actually, it is my fault. I turned so many people against him." Mr. Cogez was totally overcome with despair now, and his shoulders shook with his sobs.

Then, from the front came a sleepy moan. Startled, Mr. Cogez turned to look. The two bodies under the covers were moving.

"They are alive!" exclaimed the miller.

"Oh, yes, they are alive," said the pastor. He had not been startled when they awoke as had the miller. "But I am certain they are extremely hungry. My wife is fixing them a hot Christmas breakfast in the parsonage kitchen."

"I am so thankful they did not freeze to death, sleeping in this old church all night." As Mr. Cogez spoke these words, the pastor could hear the relief in his voice.

"Yes. For some reason I felt compelled to check the church just after midnight," the pastor explained. "I found the two of them sleeping. It was so cold that I was afraid they would freeze to death. Since they seemed so exhausted, rather than rouse them I just covered them with a woolen blanket and started a fire in the stove. They never moved."

Shock over the near tragedy and the way Nello and Patrasche had been put out of their hut quickly spread through the little village that bright Christmas Day. News of the change in Mr. Cogez also spread. Although he was greatly responsible for all the misery caused to Nello and his family, the townspeople could not excuse themselves. They had listened to the rumors and had been easily swayed to follow Mr. Cogez's example. Responsibility lay at every doorstep.

They had all known of the sad conditions in which the old man, the boy, and the faithful dog were forced to live; but not one of them had lifted a hand to provide relief. Yes, they felt guilty, and rightly they should; for even at a time of year when generosity overflowed to friends and relatives, not one had considered providing Nello with a hot meal. Every shopkeeper and merchant had seen the shabby, threadbare clothes Nello wore, yet they chose to ignore his need. Now they were ashamed of their selfishness. They had been concerned only with making their own lives more comfortable. They had turned their backs on responsibility and had forgotten God's commands to care for the poor and needy. To them, Nello, his great-grandfather, and especially the old, useless dog were someone else's responsibilities.

## *A VISITOR*

The day after Christmas, a visitor came from Antwerp to the little village. He was an admired and respected artist who had been one of the judges of the art contest. He had admired Nello's work, but his fellow artists had outvoted him.

"I am looking for the young man who should have won the prize in the art contest in Antwerp the day before Christmas," he announced in the little shops. "He has rare promise and genius. His drawing was so simple—just an old woodcutter at dusk, sitting on a fallen tree. Whoever drew that picture has a great future ahead of him, and I am prepared to help him. I will teach him more about art, for he obviously has a God-given talent."

At first, no one in the little village seemed to know whom the artist wanted to find. When word reached the mill house, Alois said, "The artist must be looking for Nello. He loves to draw, as you know, Father."

Mr. Cogez sent for the artist and took down the piece of pine that had been above the kitchen fireplace. He showed it to the artist and asked, "Do you think the same person might have drawn this picture?"

The artist looked at it carefully and smiled. "I am sure of it. It has the same rough but beautiful shading. It captures a moment rather than merely showing a picture. Where is the boy? I must meet him. He has a rare gift."

Alois was nearly bursting with joy for her friend. All that Nello had said seemed to be coming true. He truly had a gift, and someone with influence had noticed. She also saw the pride with which her father had shown the little piece of pine to the artist. Just as Nello had predicted, her father was no longer ashamed of him.

"He is at the parsonage of the old, gray church across the street," said Mr. Cogez. "I will take you to him."

"The young man is a pastor's son?" asked the man from Antwerp.

"No, he is not the pastor's son. He is just staying there for now." Then the miller went on to tell of the misery, mistreatment, and grief Nello had suffered in his short life.

The events of the next few days moved quickly. The artist, true to his word, arranged to take Nello to his home in Antwerp and train him to be an artist. He agreed to take Patrasche also.

On his last Sunday in the village, Nello, faithful as always, responded to the toll of the old belfry bell. He was not alone. All the villagers came, led by the miller and his family. God had given them another opportunity, and they gratefully sought His forgiveness. The church could hardly hold the people, and the pastor preached with more fervor than ever. His words reached down and exposed the ugly truths that were buried in cold hearts. The people had turned their backs on God's needy children. Selfishness had blinded them. Greed had overcome responsibility. Now repentance must replace sin.

"Who is your neighbor?"

The words pierced hearts and seemed to echo over the white winter fields and follow the frozen canals to the dikes holding back the wild North Sea.

The warm sunshine of God's love and forgiveness can melt the coldest hearts and bring spiritual renewal. Change occurred as willing souls responded to God's question, "Who is your neighbor?" Godly actions witnessed to His work in their hearts. God's love truly touched the little Flemish village that lay outside Antwerp, and even the casual observer could not miss it.

The two landmarks of the village remained—the windmill and the old, gray church. The windmill continued to grind in fits and starts, faithfully serving the needs of the community. The old, gray church, however, which for so long had been neglected, took on a new appearance. The stained-glass windows were repaired. The moldy stones were scrubbed until they shone. The heavy double doors got a coat of welcoming paint. As the bell in the little steeple pealed passionately each Sunday morning, those

who had once turned their backs on other members of God's family now hurried to the old landmark. They rejoiced in God's forgiveness and gladly claimed as their own the once shabbily dressed boy, whose greatest desire was to use his talent to serve God.

In the years that followed, paintings began to cover the walls inside the old, gray church. The pictures showed the same simplicity and shading as had those of a little girl and dog in a meadow and an old woodcutter on a fallen tree. However, these paintings portrayed a Saviour with little children, a child being raised from the dead, a blind man receiving his sight, and other scenes that captured a long-ago moment. Yet, the greatest masterpiece was the one engraved on the hearts of the villagers. There the true Artist had captured the love of I Corinthians 13.

Eventually two tombstones appeared in the little graveyard at the side of the old church. Both often received a visitor, whom the villagers noted had grown to manhood. He left many flowers and tears there. And the two tombstones? One honored a loving great-grandfather, and the other—strange as it may seem—bore only the name "Patrasche."